Paddlepuss Does a Runner

Jan Leader
Illustrations Darren Goleby

All characters appearing in this work are fictitious. Any resemblance to real persons, living or dead, is purely coincidental.

Published by Boolarong Press,
655 Toohey Road
Salisbury Qld 4107
Australia.
www.boolarongpress.com.au

First published 2017

Cataloguing-in-Publication entry available at the National Library of Australia

Creator: Leader, Jan, author.

Title: Paddlepuss does a runner / Jan Leader ; illustrated by Darren Goleby.
ISBN: 9781925522211 (paperback)

Target Audience: For primary school age.
Subjects: Platypus--Juvenile fiction.
Fairies--Juvenile fiction.
Children's stories, Australian.
Other Creators/Contributors: Goleby, Darren, illustrator.

Printed and bound by Watson Ferguson & Company, Salisbury, Australia

Alex was staring at his shiny 20 cent piece. Little did he know staring straight back at him was Paddlepuss the platypus.

Alex and his little brother, Stru, loved looking for treasures and platypuses. Alex was rock hopping when the 20 cent piece fell from his pocket. *Bounce, bounce, splop*, it landed in the soft sand.

Paddlepuss could hardly believe his luck! He slipped off his coin; had a big stretch and a yawn, before waddling across the sand to slide quietly into the cool, clear water.

Paddlepuss playfully swam in the river ducking and diving, rumbling and tumbling, looking for others just like him.

He called out under water “blub, blub, blub”. He said in a whisper above the water “hello”. Platypuses are very shy.

Paddlepuss headed downstream in search of a friend. He floated on the top; he snuffled and rolled around on the bottom.

He scooted down a little waterfall, leapt in the air and landed with a noisy *PLOP*. "Ewwww"! he said loudly; it was smelly.

Paddlepuss stumbled through the thick, gooey, plastic mess to the bank. He noticed a man in a big noisy truck driving away as other trucks waited in a long line.

These were nasty, lazy, people dumping rubbish. Paddlepuss scrambled up over the rocks swimming as fast as he could away from that stinky pond.

As he rolled in the sand to get rid of the muddy goo, he heard a soft voice nearby. "Hello I'm Riverpuss." Paddlepuss could not believe his eyes. This was the prettiest little girl platypus he had ever seen.

Riverpuss curled up her ducky nose, "you don't smell good; are you sick?" Paddlepuss laughed,"I'm very well thank you; I was just downstream where the water is yukky".

Riverpuss was shocked, “you went down to Stinkypond; why did you do such a thing?”

“I was only there for the tiniest of whiles and will never, ever be going back!” said Paddlepuss.

Sadly, river and fairy folk no longer go there. It was a beautiful billabong long, long ago. Paddlepuss suddenly shouted, "Oh no! oh no! my coin is lost; no I am lost, oh goodness me what will I do now?"

Riverpuss was a very clever platypus. She knew exactly what to do. "Follow me; quickly, we must swim upstream and find my fairy friends. They'll know how to find your coin."

"Will they help me?" he asked sadly.

"Yes, yes, silly billy they love to help others, but they will want a favour in return."

Off they hurried upriver, joyfully scooting and snooping in search of the fairies. Riverpuss clambered from the water shaking herself like a wet puppy. "Hello is anyone there?"

In reply a tiny lispy voice could be heard. “Yeth, in fact there are theveral anyone’ths here.” Fairies in this area were known for their lilty lisp and enchanting water dancing.

A teensy mauve fairy floated above the water; another fairy sat nearby on her baby poatee, while just above hovered a river fairy who looked like an itsy-bitsy insect to adults.

The wee poatee was perfectly formed, neither goat nor pony, simply poatee. Whilst poatees are minikin and wonderful to look upon, they are a thousand times stronger than a full-sized pony.

Introductions exchanged, Paddlepuss explained his dilemma. Then, *poof!* the fairies left without a word, so back into the river the platypuses went for more rollicking and frolicking.

The little poatee flew swiftly towards the riverbank landing effortlessly with a large coin in his saddlebag. The fairies following were zigging for observing and zagging just for fun.

Shuffling towards his coin, Paddlepuss waved goodbye. Arms folded, river fairy said, "Uh aah, don't forget you owe uth a favour".

"I'm so sorry, how can I repay you?"

"Teach children to love nature not destroy it."

The boys were approaching… Fairies waved madly as they flew away. Paddlepuss leapt onto his coin having just enough time to blow a cheeky kiss to Riverpuss. He then snuggled into position just below the number twenty.

Stru spotted the coin; picked it up; dunked it into the water for a quick rinse before handing it to Alex to put safely back in his pocket.

Pleased to see Paddlepuss, the other coinees asked where he had been and what he had seen.

“Shhh I have an important story to tell.”

Some facts about the Platypus

The platypus is a mammal.

A mammal is an animal that nurses its young with milk.

It weighs between 0.7 Kg to 2.4 Kg

It is between 43 cm to 50 cm long.

When it dives in water it closes its nose, ears and eyes.

The platypus and the echidna are the only mammals that lay eggs.

The male platypus can deliver a venomous injection from a spur in the hind limbs.

It has electro-receptors in its bill to find its direction and its prey under water.

It is found along the east coast of Australia, including Tasmania.

The platypus lives in the water and on land.